Toby's Adult Misadventures

Jade Gace

Published by Jade Gace, 2024.

TOBY'S ADULT MISADVENTURES

First edition. January 23, 2024.

ISBN: 979-8224555543

Written by Jade Gace.

Table of Contents

To all those in and out of the closet, wardrobe and everything in between!

Be you and be beautiful!

Toby the blusher

Toby could feel something in the pit of his stomach that something was not right about today. His eyes opened quickly as he scanned around the room without moving a muscle, hearing out anything that could be the problem. Once he knew it was clear, it was time to get up which was going to be an effort. The overwhelming cramp that built up on his back was not helped by the added weight of his wings. For a bat, this was a essential part of him but some days they were his biggest burden.

His ear flicked as he could hear the post box having a fit with, for him no doubt, was more bills and other amazing surprises for him to read. Junk mail. Oh boy!

Swinging his legs to the end of the bed, Toby scratched his side and yawned before heaving himself up and walking his way into the bathroom. One mirror look and he was dreading the day. His brown fur on his head was unkempt where he'd been rolling around wrapped in his wings in his sleep. His eyes had crusts in them which he immediately wiped away revealing two very tired brown eyes staring back at him. He made a face at himself, chuckling at his childishness.

After doing what he needed to do, it was time to get dressed and have coffee. He almost broke his neck getting down stairs as the urge for coffee was the full motivation he needed to get ready to go to work.

Before he even got to the coffee pot, his phone rang.

"Goddamnit!!

With a frustrated sigh, Toby took his phone from his phone and pressed a button "Yo, what's up?"

"You awake yet? You got to get to work as soon as possible Toby."

Ah, the familiar voice of his work friend, Dusty. Toby and Dusty were the most unlikely friends since Toby was a small 5ft something tall bat and Dusty... he was built like a brick house at 6ft 6 and was a bull. An unusual friendship but they helped each other out with things. That's all Toby needed.

And the motivation to get going of course.

"Toby? You up?"

Toby sighed "I am, just getting ready to go now."

"Oh good, see you in five minutes then?"

"Sure."

Toby looked lovingly at his coffee pot with a sigh. *Goodbye my love.* He quickly put on his jacket before opening his door, locking it behind him and flew off to work which was only a few blocks away.

Dusty noticed the dishevelled Toby coming into the café as he let out a smile to his friend "Toby, you're here! Nice to see you bright and early for once!"

Toby made a face at him "Huh?"

Dusty laughed "Only kidding! Anyway, big boss said that we have to get set up for today; it's gonna be a big one!"

Toby sighed rolling his eyes "Oh the joy..." he hastily put on his dark green work apron on and started cleaning to prepare for the first customers.

A beautiful white furred poodle came into the café and looked around in curiosity. She smiled towards Dusty who gave her a nod before going up to the counter where Toby was busy sorting out cups and glasses.

"Excuse me sir," she said towards him as he looked over his shoulder and noticed the young girl. A deep blush came to his cheeks as he became tongue tied and stuttered, hiding his face again. Dusty let out a hearty laugh.

"Don't worry 'bout him, miss. He gets nervous in front of cute ladies."

The poodle girl blushed as Toby shot Dusty a death stare, only making the bull laugh harder at his friend. The poodle let out a small giggle as Toby turned around completely, avoiding her gaze as he scratched the back of his neck.

"So... um... What would you like?"

The poodle girl placed her arm on the counter and rest her head on it. "I was hoping for a cup of coffee but your number wouldn't be too bad either, bat boy."

Toby blush went from deep blush to almost blood red. He was practically stuttering his words now and became a blubbering mess, even Dusty couldn't stop chuckling. Toby did as he was told and made the poodle some coffee with some effort of trying not to die of embarrassment in the process. At the same time, he almost dropped the cup in his hand a number of times and had a near miss with the coffee scalding him completely. The underwhelming feeling of embarrassment was still etched on Toby's face as he trundled his way back to the counter and handed the coffee over.

"Here. Coffee. Lady." It all he could say to her. The poodle smiled and took her coffee from him. She gave him a wink.

"I think I'm going to come here a lot more often," she said as she sashayed out of the café with her order. Toby couldn't help but look ahead of him in a blushing stupor as he heard Dusty's booming laugh. This snapped Toby out of his stupor and back to earth.

"Oh good god…"

Dusty put a strong arm around his friend "C'mon Toby! Ya did well there just got a little embarrassed, that's all! Happens to the best of us."

Toby wanted to die right there and then. He cursed himself with not being able to speak to the female species of all types without sounding like a blubbering mess but his brain and mouth seemed to work in two different ways. Plus the fact he had no idea how to move like a decent person in front of a woman. Today wasn't helping him at all.

"Crap."

Dusty shook his head as he got back to his work, leaving his friend to it. Toby served another customer, this time a little more professionally without dropping a thing, and lucky the old boy found the young bat amusing.

"Scrawny aren't ya, for such a small lad?"

"Nah, I can't grow muscle very well, got any suggestions? Know any good gardening tips?"

The old boy just laughed at the young bat's antic as he sipped his coffee in peace. Toby went back to the counter and relaxed for a bit. Dusty gave his friend a nod as another girl came in but Toby was prepared and dragged his large bull friend to serve her.

"Dusty, your go!"

Dusty chuckled towards his friend "Not ready for a next round Toby? No problem! Just make sure everything else is cleaned out at back."

"Sure."

Toby went at the back of the café and breathed a sigh of relief. Today was sure gonna drag. For Toby, it was quite a big thing for himself being able to speak to the ladies. Sure he needed some work, but this takes time, right? He hoped so as well.

The end of the day fizzled down as Toby wiped down the tables with a damp cloth and noticed Dusty getting ready to go. Dusty was waiting for the young bat to get his things as Toby finished up and removed his apron, hanging it up.

"Pretty eventful day, huh?" Dusty smiled as he breathed in the fresh evening air, walking Toby down to where he lived. Toby let out a small shrug.

"Eh, could be worse."

Dusty let out a sly smile "Kinda like the poodle girl you blushed at, eh?"

Toby looked at his friend with a scowl. A dusting of pink started to show on his cheeks "Don't..."

Dusty laughed at him "Don't worry Toby, I thought it was pretty sweet."

Toby rolled his eyes at his friend as he stuffed his hands in his pocket "I am getting better at the whole talking to girl's thing... I just..."

"Fucked it up?" Dusty offered an answer.

"Eh."

"Dude, sometimes I get nervous with girls, we've all been there. You just gotta get some confidence."

Toby looked at Dusty in confusion "How? I've never seen you get embarrassed about a girl Dusty."

Dusty laughed "Yeah, I've been where you've been Toby; nervous as hell, blushing my ass off, the whole shebang! It's all about how you present yourself in front of the ladies."

Toby tilted his head to the side, closing his eyes briefly before opening them in a thoughtful manner. Dusty thought about something.

"Tell ya what," Dusty smiled "I was thinking about going to a bar I like to drink at and wanted to invite you to have a drink there with a few pals of mine. Whaddya say?"

Toby thought about it. If it meant he got a drink, he was done with it. That, and spending some time with his friend would be nice too.

"Sure, I'll go." Toby said reluctantly.

"You sure? I know what you're like with other people around," Dusty said with a small smile. Toby shrugged.

"Beats me being at home doing shit all, don't it? A drink sounds good too."

Dusty beamed "Fantastic, I'll call you up when you're ready tomorrow!"

Toby smiled, "Sure thing." Dusty patted Toby's shoulder in friendship before he made his way to his home a few houses down. Toby went into his house and locked the door.

Today had been one of them days but he was happy to find himself becoming that little closer to being confident. Dusty was right. It was all about confidence.

Maybe tomorrow will be a better day.

Toby's barscapade and lucky love

"Shit."

Toby couldn't find a decent shirt that he could wear that would look good enough to go to a bar to with Dusty and a few other friends that he was familiar with but not as close to. He was hopeful that he could at least try and make the effort to look good and make a new friend. He was also hopeful that he wouldn't make an ass of himself at the same time, secretly praying that there would be no pretty girls to turn him into a pile of blubbering mush.

Hopeful being the keyword here.

He sniffed a red gingham shirt he'd only wore once and decided that it didn't smell too much like an armpit to wear. Added to this was a white sleeveless shirt underneath and a pair of blue rinse jeans. He was about to put on his boots on when his phone rang, and he almost broke his neck trying to get to it and not trip on his feet at the same time.

"He- shit! Hello?"

Dusty was on the phone "Toby, you okay bud? Ya sound a little breathless."

"Stupid fucking... boot!"

"Hey, I can always phone back..."

Toby let out a large groan before answering "Nah, I'm good," he relaxed himself before speaking "What's up?"

"Just wondering if you're ready," Dusty replied to him as Toby quickly grabbed his jacket and started to lock his door behind him.

"Just out of the door now, I'll be there in about... ten minutes? Hopefully?"

Dusty chuckled "Sure thing man! Just wanted to know if you were okay with all this, I know what you're like with crowds and all that shit."

Toby started to fly "Well... I'll be fine Dusty."

"Cool, see you in a bit."

The call ended as Toby flew over a few buildings towards the bar that Dusty and a few others were hanging around. Whilst he was flying, Toby decided to look around for a bit, not only to calm his nerves but to just see what the night sky can do to where he lived.

Most of it was a shithole... garbage cans everywhere, the ripe smell of rotten food and trash that enveloped his nostrils but somehow beyond all the drama, Toby could feel the comfort in this. The corner store with the old Duck lady who had a thing for him every time he went in there. The local takeaway run by the two sheep brothers who were not from around here but Toby had a fascination with and liked to talk to them about where they were from.

This ended sooner rather than later as Toby approached the bar his friend was currently standing outside with alongside some others. Dusty noticed his friend in the air and waved at him as he landed.

"Hey Toby."

Toby nodded towards him friend, noticing Dusty's other friends behind him and giving a shy nod towards them as well. One of them, a stag gave him a smile.

"Nice to meet you, Toby, Dusty's mentioned you quite a bit to us."

"Nothing bad, I hope," Toby looked suspiciously at Dusty who looked shocked.

"I would never!"

The group laughed which made Toby relax more as they entered the bar and went to sit down on the stools. Toby sighed as he sat down, taking in the smell of alcohol in the air and the strange musty smell that emanated naturally from the atmosphere. He would've kept this persona up but a light blush came on his cheeks as one of Dusty's friends, surprisingly another bat, sat with him.

"Hi," She smiled towards him "my name's Felicia."

"Um..."

"Don't worry, Dusty told me that you get nervous with girls."

"Right." Toby fumbled a bit but still mustered up enough courage to speak "Would you like... a drink? I'll pay."

Felicia smiled "Sure!"

Toby ordered two drinks as they started to talk for a while and they surprisingly got along very well. The booze worked its magic on Toby as he became more talkative towards Felicia and he found himself becoming more attracted to her. Her snow white fur. Big blue eyes. He was worried of looking too much of a creep in front of her and looked away from time to time, Felicia also doing the same.

It only stopped when they both heard a noise coming from the door and out walked in a warthog and his mini gang, consisting of a rhino, a pig and hippo. One of the guys, the rhino, happened to sit right next to Toby.

Toby's head turned a little and noticed the ungodly sight of the Rhino's body. Asides from his obese weight, the large denim vest jacket he wore with an assortment of badges and the ripped jeans and boots, the rhino had pierced nipples peeking out from the jean vest. Of all the things Toby imaged and had stared at.

"Help Felicia…"

Felicia tilted her head "What's up Toby?"

Toby swallowed "Have you seen the size of this guy's nipples?"

Felicia let out a loud laugh before she covered her mouth with her hand, simmering it down to a small chuckle "Toby!"

Toby let out a snicker "C'mon, they're nearly the size of a dinner plate! I'm scared I'll turn my head and he'd slap me with one of his tits…"

Felicia was in the middle of a drink before she spat it out in laughter. The rhino looked concerned.

"Hey girl, you okay?"

Felicia kept her gaze away from his body to his face and nodded "Yeah, I'm fine. Don't worry."

The rhino nodded before getting back to his drink. Toby and Felicia looked at each other and giggled like two teenagers. The buzz of alcohol was doing wonders for Toby's confidence plus the fact he was sharing a laugh with a girl he'd somehow become friendly with. Dusty looked over towards Toby and Felicia and let out a small smile towards the two. Seeing Toby like this was nice and Toby with a girl was even better, albeit pumped up with booze.

"Just going to the bathroom, I'll be right back," Toby said towards Felicia who nodded towards him, watching him walk over to the men's room with some effort whilst bumping into a few chairs in the process, making her giggle. She could feel someone behind her and noticed the pig behind her.

"Um, hi?"

The pig snorted "Hey gorgeous... just wondering if a beautiful lady such as yourself wanted to have a drink with a hunk like myself?"

"No thanks," replied Felicia who took a sip of her drink. The pig snorted again before resting himself in front of her.

"C'mon girl, I can show you a good time."

Felicia's nose curled in disgust as she noticed Toby coming out of the bathroom and looked over towards her. Her face said it all. *Help me!*

" 'Scuse me good sir, are you trying to make a move on my girl?" Toby asked with as much dignity as he could without looking like he was drunk. It was failing a bit with the swaying he was doing, plus the slur in his voice did not help him either.

The pig softened "Oh shit, sorry lady! Didn't know you had a guy! Jus' that you were alone an' all..."

Felicia stopped him "Don't worry about it." She stood up and went over to Toby, hooking her arm around him and resting her head on his shoulder, "Toby, I think we'd better get you home, shouldn't we?"

Toby could only nod as a blush made itself known on his cheeks. Today just got better. Felicia was nice enough to phone a cab for Toby and offered to pay for him to get home. Dusty went over to Toby and smiled.

"Dude, I can't believe you totally stood up for Felicia... That was real brave of ya, bud!"

Toby shrugged his shoulders, wobbling and swaying on his feet "Jus' done what any good guy does."

"Still, that was kinda brave of ya... guy looked pretty tough for a pig"

Toby brushed Dusty's comment "Prolly... Bacon's just bacon, right?"

Dusty shook his head "seriously, how drunk are ya?"

Toby let out a cheeky smile before he indicated with his thumb and forefinger "Jus' a smidge."

Dusty let out a laugh as he helped his friend into the cab and shut the door. The cab driver let out a giggle "Long night, eh?"

"Not too bad, good mister... jus' wanna get home now."

The cab driver was a good person and had a laugh with Toby as he drove him home in good time. Toby struggled up to his door as he swayed and managed with enough dignity to open the door and let himself in. Nearly breaking more bones in his body, he made it upstairs to get ready for bed.

Toby's luck in love

Felicia started to talk to Toby a lot more since the bar incident and they started to get to know each other a lot better, this time without the booze doing the talking for Toby. He found himself becoming talkative with her without feeling like an idiot and, for him, it was nice to be able to laugh again with her.

"I can't believe that the guy's nipples were the first thing you thought of, Toby," Felicia giggled as she settled her arm on Toby's as they walked down the street. Toby let out a laugh.

"Seriously... the size of 'em didn't help me either, they were like dinner plates! I swear the guy needed a bra, maybe a size 34DD."

Felicia laughed "Toby!"

Toby laughed "To be honest, that would kill me off more if he was wearing a bra, not that I'm against anyone's fashion sense or what they choose to wear, that's up to them. I just couldn't help look and notice 'em swinging about the place."

Felicia laughed as she held onto Toby's arm with her other hand and rest herself on his shoulder like the other day. Toby smiled at her as they continued their walk.

"Did you really mean it when you said that I was your girl?" Felicia asked him.

Toby let out a blush "Well... it was the only way to get the creepy pig guy away from you. Lucky enough that he was a gentleman though, I was worried about my teeth being smashed in."

Felicia looked up at him "So it was to save me then? What a hero you've turned out to be."

Toby let out a cheeky smile "A terrified hero but a hero nonetheless."

Felicia giggled as they arrived at the café and went in. Dusty noticed the couple as they sat down at a table.

"Hey guys, fancy seeing you here," he smiled towards them as Toby blushed a pink colour and Felicia smiled towards him.

"Dude, really?" Toby muttered.

"We just came here for some coffee Dusty, that's all," Felicia said towards him as he nodded to get some coffee for them both. As he was doing this, Felicia and Toby started chatting against themselves again.

"So do you have any family?" asked Toby towards Felicia as she nodded towards him.

"Mom and a sister... not too sure about my dad though since he left when me and my sister were young but my family has been great growing up. Mom was always the one picking up the pieces when shit was real"

Toby nodded "Better than what I have. Me and my brother and sister were brought up partly by our mom when we were younger but she was a little unhinged. Not a nice person to be near. We went to our uncle after a while who was the best person in the world and still is. Made sure we had what we needed with no trouble."

Felicia nodded as Dusty came over with the coffees and set them down in front of them. He nudged Toby on his side and winked. The deadpan look on Toby's face said it all.

Piss off, I'm busy!

Dusty let out a deep chuckle as he let the couple to it. Felicia placed on elbow on the table and rest her head on her hand "So, what are you into? Anything in particular that you like to do when you're not at work?"

Toby thought about it "Video gaming? I know that sounds a bit typical but it's a great stress reliever. More of an First Person Shooter kind of guy but I like playing anything. That and I like to draw as well, both traditional and digital. Little bit of graphic design. I wanna get into creating comics but I haven't got that much patience or time."

Felicia nodded "Don't worry, I like video games but I can't draw that well. I like writing though..." Toby lit up when she said that "I also enjoy photography as well but I'm still learning how to use photo editing software."

"That's cool."

It was nearly closing by the time Toby and Felicia stopped their chatting. The amount of coffee cups scattered on their table suggested that they had one of the best chat sessions, or they were addicts in need of their caffeine. During this, the couple didn't realise how much time had passed until Dusty came over to stop their chat.

"Guys, we're almost closing up so I hope you are ready to go."

Felicia looked at her phone "Shit! I totally didn't notice the time!" she stood up just as Toby did and smiled at him.

"Thanks for today Toby, I had a lot of fun."

Toby let out a small smile "No problem Felicia."

Felicia paused as she went over to him and held his hand. She looked into his eyes and leaned in and kissed him on the mouth. The look on Toby's face was priceless and it took a lot of effort for Dusty not to burst out laughing.

Toby could feel his blood pressure going into over drive and his head getting dizzy but it stopped after Felicia removed her lips from his. He had two options: return the favour or flop on the floor like a fish.

Just as Felicia turned to go, Toby took her hand. She looked at him as he quickly leaned into her lips and kissed her back. Like a shy school boy, he withdrew his hand and blushed a bright crimson.

"So, see you soon?" he asked, feeling hopeful and very hot.

"Sure," Felicia smiled as she made her way out of the café. As soon as she as gone, Toby's fish flop came into place and he was on the verge of fainting as Dusty caught him.

"Whoa there!"

Toby's eyes were closed as a big smile went on his face. A warm feeling in his chest bloomed as he could only think of the girl that he chatted on for hours with. And the kiss.

Ah, the kiss.

Dusty snapped his fingers in front of Toby "Toby, you okay?"

"Yeah pretty lady, I'm feeling fine and dandy," Toby said through his delusional phase as he snapped out of it, noticing Dusty's face looking down at him. His face looked disgusted at him.

"Oh good god!"

Dusty grunted at him "You idiot... you okay now?"

"Yeah," Toby let out a small smile "just dandy."

Dusty shook his head at his friend. Despite the little mishap, Dusty was proud of him for being able to step out of his comfort zone.

Dusty's sex education

Dusty was a little more confident with the ladies than his friend was. Whilst he was not a casa nova, he knew how to charm and treat a girl right. This meant in and out of the bedroom, not that he had the guts to admit the latter.

He'd met a lady called Denise at a bar and agreed with her to have a no strings attached relationship with her. If they wanted a hook up, either of them were down for it. It was just a text or phone call away and they'd got down to business.

Can't wait to see you tonight, baby...

Me neither sexy...

Dusty's only thing was the reaction that Toby would have if he'd mentioned this to his friend. Dusty thought Toby would look at him different, freaked out? Maybe a little bit disgusted?

Toby relaxed on his friend's sofa and had a beer with him. He was surprised with the whole relationship that he was undertaking with this cow woman since, to him, Dusty seemed the guy to be committed to a relationship with the one girl.

"So you and her get together like once a month to get it on with her?" Toby was intrigued by the whole set up his bull friend arranged after it was explained to him. Dusty nodded.

"Pretty much."

"Didn't take you as that kind of guy." Toby smirked as he took a swig of his drink. Dusty rolled his eyes at his friend.

"I'm just a little more private about my love life, unlike you," Dusty snorted as Toby shrugged his shoulders at his friend.

"That was one time," Toby paused to sip his drink "my first time."

Dusty snorted again" So have you and Felicia done it?"

The beer Toby was consuming now made an impressive fountain from his nose as he snorted and coughed. A bight blush came on Toby's face alongside the beer fountatin. Dusty laughed at him.

"Guess that's a no then," he took a small sip of beer.

"No, of course not!" Toby finally spoke without snorting as he placed his bottle on the table. "I want to take things slow and she does as well."

"Are you scared? It's okay if you are, you're not exactly 'experienced' if you don't mind me saying," Dusty said. Toby rolled his eyes, finishing his bottle and got himself another one.

"Don't rub it in."

"If you want, I can teach you a little about the birds and the bees, if you know what I mean," Dusty said with a cheeky smile. Toby was unimpressed with his friend as he opened his beer bottle.

"I know how it all goes, Dusty."

Dusty took a deep breath and started to explain "When a man and a woman are in love, they want to show it in many ways. Dinner dates, movie dates, kissing, cuddling, all the mushy stuff that you see in romantic novels and movies."

"Oh boy." Toby sighed as he prepared himself for the lecture. There was no stopping Dusty when he started his mini lectures.

"There is another way a man and a woman show each other love and that is through sexual intercourse," Dusty continued, ignoring the small giggle coming from Toby at his rather dramatic explanation.

"Sorry," Toby tried to stop his giggle "You're such a drama queen when you lecture."

Dusty let out a sigh "Anyway, both the man and the woman get undressed whilst caressing each other in each other's arms as they... you know, prepare themselves for the whole act."

"Foreplay?" Toby said bluntly. Dusty looked at his friend.

"Yes, Foreplay... and there are certain things that a man does to prepare his woman for the act involving a lot of things to do with his hands and..." Dusty paused, feeling a bit embarrassed.

"His mouth?" Toby suggested, earning a small smack on his shoulder from Dusty as he laughed.

"I do not!"

"Then why are you blushing?" Toby laughed, pointing at him.

Dusty wiped his wet nose with his hand as he continued "Some instances involve a man's mouth but mostly his hands. Anyway, there are some cases a woman will do things to a man as well with her hands..."

"And her mouth..." Toby couldn't help add it in to see his friend blush again. He earned another slap on his shoulder as he laughed at Dusty.

"Give or take. Anyway, this all goes on for some time before they are both ready to start the act of sexual intercourse where the man goes inside a woman."

"You mean, ploughs her silly?"

Dusty sighed.

"Bangs her silly?"

Dusty grumbled.

"Shoots the hoop?"

Another death glare from Dusty just made Toby laugh. Quite clearly the beer was going to his friend head so he dismissed his friend's comments.

"The man enters the woman or vice versa until they both climax."

"Ah, an orgasm... gotcha!"

Dusty shook his head, "Yes, that too" Dusty let out a small sigh which turned into a slight moo. Toby couldn't stop himself from laughing at his friend about something as Dusty looked over towards him.

"What are you giggling at now?"

"That sigh you did just now... is that the noise you make when you orgasm?" Toby laughed out loud as Dusty shook his head towards his friend.

"Very funny "Mister inexperienced"... at least you get the idea on what happens if you plan to do anything with Felicia."

"I said I am taking it slow, not like my first time; that was hasty judgement to get laid," Toby admitted as he took a swig of beer from his bottle. Dusty was surprised from Toby's comment but made no effort to speak. He turned to his friend and spoke.

"You used protection, don't you?"

Toby nodded "Yeah, I had condoms when I first did it and I'm defiantly going to use them again. I ain't that stupid."

Dusty was going to say something but decided not to, saving his face. Toby wondered something about his friend and decided to ask him about something on his mind.

"Do you?"

Dusty looked at Toby "Hm?"

"Do you use protection? You know, with the lady friend you have on the side?"

Dusty nodded "I always do! Nothing nasty is coming out of either of us and I make sure that I get tested for anything horrible either. I even ask if she can too."

"Cool." Toby smiled towards his friend. Dusty seemed happy to be able to share this with Toby and have a good laugh about this. Their friendship was a strange one but it worked between them both. It suited them both.

The beers were drunk and the two boys relaxed for a while as the quiet around them was soothing. Dusty noticed Toby on his phone for a bit, texting away as Dsuty took out his own to text his lady-friend, Denise.

Hey honey, just checking up on ya. Wanted to know if you're up to anything?

It took a while for a text to come back.

Nothing much baby, just working. Will see you soon though for our night together xxx

Dusty let out a smile at his phone, not noticing the young bat across from him staring at him. The change in Dusty was different when he was on his phone, not that Toby minded. It was a little weird to know this secretive side of his friend but he supported him.

To each there own, as they say.

Felicia's misadventure with Zara

Toby had no idea that Felicia had a friendship with the poodle girl he'd badly blushed in front of the other day when she'd come in for a coffee. Likewise, he never got the girls name either which sucked for him but made a great memory nonetheless for the young poodle girl he'd tried (and failed) to chat with. Zara reminisced this with Felicia as she started to laugh about Toby's moment when Zara flirted with him.

"Poor Toby" she smiled as Zara giggled.

"He was cute though when he was blushing towards me afterwards but I did worry about him fainting," Zara said as she continued "It was lucky the bull guy was there to pick him up."

"Yeah, I met Toby through Dusty actually. We were going to a bar when I met him." Felicia mentioned as Zara's brown eyes grew big.

"So, what was he like with you?"

"He was a little shy but we got on well... I don't think it helped with the beer he was consuming either but he was really sweet," Felicia remembered a particular part that made her giggle which confused Zara.

"What?"

"There was an incident where I swear I have never have laughed so much in my life," Felicia said in between giggling.

"C'mon! Tell me!" insisted Zara.

"Okay, so one guy in particular came in, big rhino guy that was built like a house, and Toby really could not help but talk about the guys nipples all the way through!"

"What?" Zara tilted her head towards her friend "That's weird."

"If you were there Zara, you would've said the same thing Toby did. The guy did have big boobs and his nipples were pretty hanging low fruit, if you know what I mean" grinned Felicia with a wink.

Zara made a face that suggested she didn't want to know more as the girls made their way to the store to get something to eat. They decided to have a quick browse around the clothes section of the store as well for anything new.

As they were looking around, Felicia noticed someone familiar that was hanging around the ladies section of the store. It was the rhino guy!

"What the hell?" Felicia was surprised to see him in this particular section. Zara was a little confused but saw the expression on Felicia's face as this guy being the one that she and Toby saw the other day. She too also noticed the hulking rhino and his dainty shopping basket draped on his arm.

"Hey! You're that lady I saw the other day!"

The rhino looked over towards Felicia as she noticed him dressed in a rather short yellow t-shirt, a pair of white knee high shorts and a pair of black sneakers. In his hand was a basket of items, all of which made Felicia question what the man was doing with a pair of tights, a bra and some lace underwear.

"Um... hi?" Felicia gave the rhino man a small wave.

He came over to the two girls with a smile "Sorry 'bout my friend trying it out on you, he didn't know that the bat boy you were hanging with was your boyfriend."

"It's fine..." Felicia's eyes looked down at the items the gentleman had in his basket, "so what brings you here? Shopping for a lady friend or something?"

The rhino shook his head "Oh no! This is for me."

Felicia tried hard no to laugh. "Really?"

"Yeah, doing a drag act with a friend of mine coming up soon at the local gay club, just needed to get something to keep it all in, if you know what I mean," the rhino chuckled as Felicia still kept her laughter in.

"So are you?"

"100% hun! The boys know already and they're cool with it. Hippo boy's actually my partner. Maybe you should come to the show this week, bring your poodle friend and boyfriend with ya," smiled the rhino as he said his goodbyes and headed for the dress section. When he was out of ear shot, Felicia laughed her head off.

"Oh wait til Toby hears this!" she managed to say out in between her laughter. Zara was also laughing as well as she held onto Felicia for support.

"That's the guy you and Toby saw at the bar?" she asked Felicia. Felicia nodded as she calmed down.

"Yeah but who'd have thought he had such a nightlife! We should totally go to see his show! I'll ask Toby sometime tonight if he wants to."

Zara nodded "or make it a girl's night? I could do with a night out with some girlies..."

Felicia thought about it "Sure that sounds a lot like fun too!"

The girls continued their shopping as they selected their outfits for the night, out of sight and earshot of the gay rhino who, thankfully, had paid of his stuff and left the store. A few more essential items later, the girls paid for their shopping and made their way to the café for a pit stop.

Dusty was in the café, seemingly flirting with a customer. A brown coloured cow wearing a short white dress flirted back with him as she giggled at his comment.

"Maybe we should try that sometime," she purred with a slight moo towards him.

"Sounds good, honey" he flirted back. They were about to share a kiss before Dusty noticed Felicia and Zara come into the café.

"Hey ladies! How's it going?" he instantly changed his tune as the cow lady smiled and rolled her eyes playfully.

"I'll call you tonight hun."

Dusty rubbed the back of his head "Sure," he turned his attention on the poodle and bat girl "So, what brings you two here?"

"Just here for a pit stop," Felicia smiled as she looked around "Is Toby not working today?"

"Nah, not today Felicia, he's here tomorrow though," Dusty chuckled as he lead them to an empty table "So, two coffees?"

Felicia nodded "Thanks."

As Dusty went to get their coffees, Zara noticed the complete change in Dusty's personality. She decided to air out her observation.

"Didn't Dusty look a little flustered with that cow lady earlier?"

Felicia nodded "He did."

"So, do you think?"

Felicia nodded.

Zara accepted this "To each their own," she said absently. Dusty came over with the girls coffee's settling them down quickly before going back to the front of the shop to serve another customer.

"Today's been pretty eventful," Zara said with a small sip of coffee as Felicia nodded towards her friend. Possibly the most surreal day she'd had, Felicia couldn't help but think about the rhino guy she's seen. Despite the man's menacing appearance, he was an absolute gentleman.

Apparently Ollie's a lucky one

Pete admired his reflection in the mirror as he set himself up to prepare of dress rehearsal he was going to perform. His red dress was neatly primed and hung it its delicate wooden hanger next to his enormous red wig, teased to the dozen and covered in hair spray.

It was always a delicate process for him to get ready for stage as he liked to take his time, making sure every part of him felt fabulous. Of course in this line of work, a moment to yourself was rare as the backstage, rehearsal or on the night, was always teeming with life.

This made him smile though as he'd found somewhere where nobody said a word about him coming out in a negative way. They all were positive about it. Everyone in the club had a story to tell, some good and some bad, but they were all united.

A small knock on the door startled the rhino as he went over and opened the door. He looked around but found no one in front of him, a look of confusion on his face. He heard a voice "Down here, Dipshit!"

Pete looked down "Oh, hey Sadie."

Sadie was a small orange marmoset but tough as nails. She was not interested in the whole getting down and dirty but she too suffered her own problems with coming out as Ace. For her, the kids in this club were children to her.

"Have you heard any news lately on Cal? Heard he's having boyfriend trouble again."

"Haven't heard a thing, mama," the nickname Pete spoke made the marmoset smile, a name everyone called her at the club. She sighed deeply.

"When you see him next, tell 'im mama wants a word."

"Sure thing mama." Pete said as Sadie left him to it, closing the door behind her. Pete continued his preparation for rehearsal. He looked into the mirror and noticed the picture of himself and Eddy together which made him smile. He kissed his hand and gently tapped it on the picture without moving the mirror too much. As he started to apply his make-up, an interesting noise made him want to listen in.

"Oh god yes!"

Oh god no. The recipient of the noise was no doubt Ollie, one of the fellow members of the troupe Pete was in. He shook his head, trying to stop a laugh from breaking out. Ollie was pretty much horny most of the time and this time was no more different than the last. Judging by the grunts and moans, Ollie was enjoying himself and, to be honest, Pete didn't want to disturb them.

Both eyelashes pressed on before the eyeliner came on, slapped down with a bit of mascara. Voila!

The grunts got a little deeper as Pete knocked on his wall and shouted "Hope you're using lube in there, girls!"

Deep laughter ensued. This made Pete's day, the banter between them all was all jolly and fun. Not a bad word said between them. They'd been friends since they were kids.

"Shit!"

"Dammnit!"

A shuffle was heard before Pete could hear someone coming into the room. It was the guilty looking Ollie, buckling his belt.

"Bitch, you made him laugh damnnit..."

Pete laughed "Popped outta ya, did he?"

"No shit"

"Hope he didn't do that either."

Ollie rolled his eyes at his friend.

Pete smiled towards his friend "So, who's the unlucky soul this time, eh Ollie?"

"I am not telling you, girl" Ollie mock huffed as he sat down and smiled. The large lion relaxed on the chaise lounge that was in the room as he watched his friend get ready. The first person he'd told that he was gay and the one who'd never told him once he was a monster. Or that he was wrong for having these feelings.

"So, how'd you think the show will go?"

"I got no worries," the rhino smiled as he started to get dressed "Do ya mind?"

The lion grinned, "C'mon, lemme see that lil' peach"

"Geddout!"

A deep laugh later and Ollie left Pete to it. The delicate process of dressing was one of Pete's highlights and he never liked to rush on it, especially with a face full of makeup. One last adjustment to the outfit and he felt fabulous. A few more curls to the red wig and he was prepared, placing it delicately over his head like a crown. He felt fabulous!

Just in time to see Sadie giving Cal the goat a good scolding.

"So, explain to me sugar what the hell was going on between you and a customer last night, hm?"

"Mama, I just..."

"Ya know, that's not allowed right?"

"Er... guilty?"

Sadie shook her head "Not surprised with you, you dirty animal." Her attention now went to the rhino looking beautiful in front of her "Oh sweetheart, you look gorgeous!"

"Thanks mama." Pete was still polite, even in drag. He sashayed away from the argument to the back of the stage where he was going to perform. He noticed another one of the girls all dressed up too.

Dan.

Dan was a stallion but made drag look like it was delicate on him and he always tried to look his best. Frilly and pastel with just a hint of naughty. A nod of approval from Pete was the best confidence booster for Dan.

"Hello dear" he smiled towards him, planting a small kiss on the rhino's hand.

"Darling, you look stunning."

"Thank you."

They were both accompanied by Ollie who managed to get his bearing and shuffling his way to the others, dressed in his usual sultry and suggestive drag.

"Sorry I'm late."

"Darling, you're always late... another boy toy you've had your hands on?" Dan asked with an air of grace. Ollie snarled playfully in response.

"Bitch, at least I can get laid... I don't hold out unlike you."

"Different strokes for different folks, darling" the horse replied with a smile.

A small chuckle came from Ollie's throat as he patted Dan's shoulder in a friendly way "Touché, my friend."

"Caught him out with a boy toy, more like," Pete sniggered towards Ollie and Dan as Ollie rolled his eyes. Dan neighed with laughter.

"Oh dear... let's hope you didn't leave a mess, darling."

The rehearsal had finished and before long, the troupe split into their respective dressing rooms. Pete retired to his room and shut the door with a smile. A text message came up on his phone and a smile on his face lit up.

Good luck for the show, Petey

It was from his gang friends, wishing him luck. When he'd told them, they were immediately protective of him. They knew one word about this was enough to make him a target, regardless of what his appearance may look like. It was nice to have friends like that.

Another text came up on his phone as he looked.

Just texting to say that I'm proud of you babe... good luck for the show honey and show them some fire!

Pete smiled at the text from his partner, Eddy the hippo. It was weird they were in the same gang but no one ever mentioned that it was weird. It was just a normal relationship to them.

Sadie knocked on the door, a teacup clutched in her hand. "Just some tea for you," she said with a smile.

Pete smiled back "Thank you mama."

Sadie sat down on the chaise lounge and smiled at the rhino who took a sip of tea.

"Look at how much you've grown."

Pete was a little confused "What's up, mama?"

Sadie giggled "Just looking at you grown up Petey... I've known you since you were 10 years old and look at how wonderful you've become, honey... don't let anyone ever dull that light inside you, ya hear me?"

"Of course not mama, I won't."

Sadie nodded "Good."

She got of the chaise lounge and went out of the dressing room as Pete got changed into his normal wear to go home. One final look into his dressing room made him smile before he shut the door and locked it.

The show was going to be fantastic!

The glam show featuring Pete

It was the fifth time Toby got chatted up at the club and probably not his last. He'd been dragged out by Felicia and Zara to go and see a show in a local gay bar, intrigued mostly by the fact it was the rhino he took the piss out off at the bar who was apparently working there but also having a drink sounded like a good time with the girls. He could still see the image of the poor man's nipples.

A shiver went down his spine and it wasn't the alcohol talking.

Toby followed the girls to a table towards the back of the club as the entertainment came onto the stage. Toby had seen one or two drags acts in his time but these girls on stage were surprisingly funny and more interactive. Not like the dull acts who just think putting on a dress and prancing around counted.

"Darling, you look like a cactus just slapped you in the face and asked for a divorce," one of the queens said towards him in one act. Toby knew what to do and noticed the drab outfit they wore.

"Funny you say that, I didn't know your fashion sense involved garbage bags," he sassed back as the queen mocked being hurt but he saw the sly smile.

Another queen decided to have a shot at him, not realising that he'd fight back.

"Sweetheart, you've got a personality of a garbage can."

"At least I ain't wearing one."

Felicia liked the fact Toby was interactive with the whole situation and it was nice to see this side of him. Made her realise he wasn't going to be a dick to different people and he was accepting to whoever they were and how they identify as. Unlike her ex.

"Having fun?" she asked him as he looked at her.

"She needs to try harder to take the piss."

Felicia laughed at him as she looked towards Zara having a good time talking to one of the queens at the bar, ordering more drinks as well. Felicia could Zara felt more at home here than anywhere else as she was talking to a well-known trans-lady gazelle that Zara was friends with, waiting for the drinks. She came back from the bar with a slight skip in her step.

"The bar maid just told me that he is coming on tonight," she said, sitting down on the other side of the couple, handing out their drinks. Felicia nodded as Toby was a little confused at the girls.

"Who?"

"Rhino with the big nipples, me and Zara met him the other day. Just bought himself some tights, a bra and panties. Said something about a show and we were invited," Felicia explained to Toby who's eyes grew big.

"Eh?"

Felicia nodded "Don't judge a book by his cover, he's the nicest guy I've met."

Toby could only nod as he took a swig of his drink. Whilst the image of the rhino in silk panties was disturbing, he was going to take it at face value. After all, he was here for a good time and the atmosphere was great. The lights went down and a spotlight went on stage to signify the beginning of the show. The curtains came up and the sight in front of them made Toby nearly drop off his seat.

His rhino friend was followed by a horse and lion but they looked fabulous. Toby admitted that the rhino looked great dressed up, he was just shocked to find him here on this very night. Pete set his eyes on the young bat, approached Toby and sidled up to him.

"Met this little fellow at a bar once, just wondering if you got my call."

Toby swallowed as he replied with as much dignity as he could "I think I left you on voicemail, I never checked. Sorry honey."

"No prob sugar, just a little heads up next time. A little birdy told me, you're a man who likes a lil' bit of boob on a girl" Pete's eyes laid on Felicia "Your girl there told me all about your admiration for the bigger lady."

"Oh no." Toby felt himself blush.

Pete removed the top part of his dress, revealing two pasties hiding his nipples as the tassels tickled Toby's nose, making him sneeze.

"Hey lady, I think I'm allergic."

"Baby boy, don't be like that. Here." Pete then hugged Toby to his chest, resting the bat's head right where his boobs were. A little moan was heard from Toby as he wanted air from being squished in.

"Can't...breath!"

Pete let go of him and sashayed his way up to the stage again before blowing Toby an air kiss. Toby rolled his eyes at the action but there was a smile on his face. It was good fun.

After the show, Pete approached the table that Felicia, Zara and Toby sat at and had a drink with them.

"How'd you guys like the show?" Pete asked a little nervously towards the group who all agreed on the same thing.

"It was fabulous... could've done with more jokes though... some of those queens can't joke if they tried," Toby said as he took a drink.

"I did notice you had a good time bat boy."

Toby shrugged "I did."

Pete looked over towards Zara "Fancy seeing you here those, miss Zara, we were missing you."

Zara let out a small smile "I was busy for a while but I feel great now."

"Ah... that."

Zara nodded.

"Say no more honey."

Toby was confused "Huh?"

Zara looked at Toby "I... transitioned about a year ago."

"Oh..."

Zara let out a sigh "Sorry I..."

"It's cool" Toby smiled "To be honest, you look much cuter."

Zara giggled as Felicia felt a fuzzy feeling inside her.

That was real sweet of him.

Toby had a question on his mind and turned to Pete.

"How'd you come out? As gay, I mean?"

Pete took a deep breath "It wasn't with my parents, that's all I can say. I came here because someone rudely came out with it one day in my family, so I looked for somewhere to go where I didn't feel like shit."

Toby nodded.

"To be honest," Pete paused to take a drink before continuing, "Mama Sadie's been the best person in the world, hasn't said a bad word about any of us... she's had her problems too so she understood."

Just as he said that, Sadie came over to sit with "How're you doing, bat boy? I know Pete here couldn't keep his hands off ya but I just wanted to make sure if you felt uncomfortable or not?"

Toby raised a hand "Nah, I've been through weirder shit... and seen it too." He noticed a black ring on the middle of Sadie's right finger "You're Ace?"

"Yeah, I am... I'm surprised to see someone who's about the black ring," Sadie smiled towards him.

"Friend of mine is Ace too, wears a ring similar to yours," Toby shrugged. Sadie nodded as she placed a hand on Pete's shoulder.

"You're needed backstage hun, I think Ollies having trouble with the girder he's wearing and Dan's not getting anywhere with it."

Pete nodded as he stood up and smiled at the others "I better leave you all to it, got trouble out back with a friend who's probably stuck with the zipper again."

"Are you performing anytime soon?" asked Zara as Pete nodded.

"Got another show next week, if you'd like to come over again... we call it the ladies night!"

"Sounds great! We'll definitely be there!"

Saying their goodbyes, the trio decided to leave the club, ready for the next adventures.

I just wanna cuddle

Pete held onto the fabric of Ollie's garter as he instructed Dan to move the zip but he was having trouble trying to adjust himself.

"Darling, I'm telling you that the zipper is stuck."

"Hang on honey," Pete swapped over to Dan to help him with the stuck zipper, readjusting the zipper until it smoothly let go and went down. Ollie breathed a sigh of relief.

"Honey, you have no idea how nice that feels."

Pete let out a smile towards his friend "No problem Ollie." He left the two men to themselves as he made his way back to his dressing room and got his stuff together to go home. A text message appeared on his phone as he looked over and picked the tiny object up.

Just wanted to say how proud of you I am sweetie! I'll be picking you up in a few minutes so I hope you are almost ready, dear.

Pete let out a small laugh as he text quickly back.

Everything went well hun, just saw Zara today and she looks fabulous! Thanks so much for the message! Will see you soon!

Picking up his stuff, Pete flicked off the light switches and shut the door, locking it securely.

Outside, he saw his partner Eddy wait for him patiently outside beside the car as he waved to him happily.

"Sweetie!"

Eddy looked over and smiled as he saw his partner and gave him a big hug.

"Oh honey! I missed you so much!"

A quick peck on the mouth later and they both got into the car and drove off. During the ride, Pete filled Eddy in on what had happened during the show and after it.

"Met some fabulous people too, especially this strange bat fellow. He seemed a little aloof but once you got to know him, he wasn't so much an asshole as I thought he'd be."

"That's why we shouldn't judge others, my love," Eddy said "And I heard from the grapevine Zara was there too?"

"She totally was! She looks fabulous now! Such a sweetheart!"

"I'm glad she's happy now," Eddy said with a smile.

The conversation stopped as they pulled up to the house and got out, taking Pete's bag out from the boot before making their way indoors.

Shoes and coats off, the couple sat down on the sofa with large sighs.

"Feels good to be home," Pete smiled as he looked over to Eddy, his partner. The hippo had positioned himself on the sofa by resting his back on the side as he patted the space between the man's legs.

"Wanna cuddle?"

Pete let out a smile to his partner "Honey, I'm gonna need one."

He laid his head on his partner's large belly as he stretched out the rest of himself. Eddy stroked his partners head lovingly.

"Long day, huh?" Eddy asked towards Pete.

"Eh, could've been worse. As I said, the show went well so I can't complain."

Eddy let out a chuckle "You sure lead the eventful life, don't you honey?"

Pete laughed at him "That's how great stories are told, sweetie. Everyone's got one but some more than others don't like to admit theirs."

"True that." Pete agreed as he let out a loud groan of relief. He got up and leaned a lot closer to Eddy, resting his head near his partner. Eddy kissed him.

"Anything else? No other anecdotes to share?" Eddy asked him as Pete looked at him.

"I just wanna cuddle."

Eddy squeezed his boyfriend to him "You can plenty of those honey, that's what I'm here for." Pete relaxed himself as he nuzzled into his partners chest with a long sigh. Despite the weird looks the two got from those passer-by's who were uncomfortable, others just treated them like they were the couple they were.

They were a couple, just unconventionally.

The sigh of relief coming from Pete was the best noise Eddy could listen to since it meant the rhino was relaxed and comfortable. Away from the kerfuffle of his job in drag and in the bar. Just this moment between the two men was one of the best feelings in the world and meant a lot to both of them.

Knowing that Zara was okay was a big relief too since her long hiatus from the club. Eddy was happy she was much better and was living her best life.

That will teach you

The last time Toby had this much of a headache... couldn't really remember the last time. Not even the time he was at the bar, talking his guts up in front of Felicia.

"The booze," was the only thing he could muster out of his mouth before realising the bad smell emitting was from his own breath. If death had a smell, he was it.

"Shit, I stink," Toby had a scratch as he talked to himself, trying to convince himself to get up. His legs were refusing to listen to him as he felt like flopping on the floor like a demented fish from the sheer lead weight of his legs.

He'd had a good time though, last night was pretty amazing for him. He was just surprised with the open honesty of some of the people. Pete, Sadie, Zara.

She was an interesting one, Zara.

Not that it bothered him in the slightest. In honesty, Toby actually thought he'd made Zara's day by being the awkward flirt in front of her. As he was with most women apart from Felicia.

Dusty's number had come up on his phone as Toby looked over and picked up the small object.

"Hello?"

"Hey there drunky, you up?"

Toby frowned "I am up, just not physically up."

Dusty let out a laugh "Alright, just wondered when you're gonna get your ass up and get to work."

Right. Work. The place where Toby earned money.

"I'll be there in ten."

"Okay."

Dusty cut off the phone as Toby had managed to get out of bed and quickly shower, get change and rush out of the door. Flying to work was a lot quicker and it was one of the best ways that Toby could think that would clear his head of the night beforehand.

Not that it was a bad night either since he had a grand old time. Just had one too many drinks, both on and off the table.

Dusty noticed Toby flying and waved at him "Toby!"

Toby landed and quickly put on his apron "Sorry about that Dusty, had a late night last night."

Dusty nodded "No problem, just happy you're here, bud."

Toby let out a half smile as he got to work cleaning up the booths and tables with chairs. A few regular customers came in to order their beverage of the day as Toby noticed a particular couple coming in.

It was Pete.

Pete and his boyfriend?

Strange...

"Oh hi there, bat boy!" Pete waved towards Toby as Toby let out a half assed wave.

Pete went over to Toby, holding his boyfriends hand "Here's the fellow I had some fun with last night! Nice to see you again. Didn't realise that you worked here though."

"Been here a while now," Toby said as Pete and Eddy sat down at a booth. The couple held hands as Toby took care of their orders and returned with their coffee's.

"Thank you, sweet boy," Eddy said with a smile as he took a sip.

"No problem."

The couple talked amongst themselves as another customer came in and noticed the couple talking together and holding hands. The look on the ram's face told the story that he didn't agree with it.

"Ugh, look at that."

Toby could feel himself getting annoyed at the customer but maintained his straight face.

"Sir, is there something I can help you with?"

The ram looked at the young bat with a smile "Coffee please, black."

"Like your soul sir?" Toby muttered under his breath out of ear shot of the ram.

The ram wouldn't give up staring at the male couple as Pete looked over at the old man.

"Do you have a problem sir?"

The look on Pete's face told the ram to back off from whatever poisonous words they were going to spout. The ram paid for his black coffee before he trundled off out of the café, slightly terrified at the rhino.

"You took that surprisingly well," Toby said towards Pete as he had a small break. Pete let out a small snort from his nostrils.

"It annoys me sometimes," Pete explained "As much as we get a few noticing that it's sweet, there are a few that grind my gears when they cross the line."

"I noticed the look on your face," Eddy said towards Toby.

Toby was confused "Eh?"

Eddy let out a giggle "You weren't too pleased with the fellow either, were you?"

Toby shrugged "I just don't like it when people think it's disgusting when two happy folk are having a coffee together and don't fit conventions."

"Touché darling" Eddy toasted Toby with the coffee cup as he drained the rest of his drink down. Toby let out a smile.

"Would you like a refill? It's on me."

"Why, aren't you just a sweetheart?" Eddy gave Toby a sweet smile.

Toby let out a blush of embarrassment "So they tell me, sir."

Dancing with me, myself and I

Toby didn't realise that the same gay bar he'd once been chatted up by a rhino in had also hosted mini shows where there was a little bit of dancing. Of course, it was one of those things the highly confident and highly intoxicated could join in perfectly.

Lucky for them, he was becoming one but felt more like the other. Dusty was a good sport by letting Toby have a few days off so he decided to chill out in the bar without Felicia and Zara there. After getting himself acquainted with the bar tender (who happen to know Zara), he put down a few good beers before making his way to the dance floor.

Pete was there though, which was a comforting thing. At least he had his support.

"Enjoying yourself there hun?" Pete giggled as he noticed a slight intoxicated Toby have a good boogie on the dance floor. The boy couldn't dance to save his life but seeing him dancing like an idiot made him chuckle. It was more entertaining seeing this strange bat dancing than it was of the show that was going on that all eyes went on him. Not that Toby cared.

"Groovy."

Sadie couldn't stop herself from laughing at the bat as he threw a few shapes on the floor. Toby had no idea how to dance but seeing him trying his best was all she could ask for. And it was a funny sight to behold.

"Mind the table!"

Toby had narrowly missed one or two tables in his dance-o-thon, apologising to one of them. He was lucky there was no one sitting down as they were all stood up either at the bar or on the dance floor with this strange guy. This cracked Ollie up completely as the lion couldn't stop but admire the bat for trying.

"So that's the dance you chose to woo the ladies with, eh? Not too bad Mr Shoe Shuffle, you're definitely showing the rest of us girls up."

"I'm totally feeling it!" Toby shouted.

"You sure it's that or the booze talking."

Toby pinched his thumb and forefinger mid jig towards Ollie's way "Smidgen."

"I'll take that as a both then... keep on going bat boy!"

Toby didn't need to be told twice with his mini shuffles on the floor. Ollie shook his head with a smile on his face and left him to it.

Sadie decided to have a go herself and joined the solo bat on the floor with some others.

"Ooh, partner!"

Despite the height difference, they both made it work out and had a good duo jig around the floor, laughing like two teenagers. It was nice to see this side of Toby that was beginning to blossom out. Despite Pete not knowing the bat for long, he understood that he was a decent guy. Someone who you could trust.

Sadie dragged Pete up to the floor "C'mon! Join us!"

Pete let out a hearty laugh as he joined in on the good time they were having. A lot of the other queens were too busy either watching them, laughing with them or in their rooms.

Quite the busy day.

It's been a while

Zara knew it had been a year since her transitioning and it was a very eventful year as well.

The hormones, the looks and stares from those who knew her beforehand... she ploughed through the whole year taking everything on the chin and still kept her pretty little head up.

No one really knew her old name, not that it mattered to them either as she was welcomed into the whole family at the gay bar instantly. The kindness she experienced from all of the people there helped to shape who she wanted to be.

She had one particular person to thank and that was Sadie. Sadie was like a mother to her. As soon as she'd found out about Zara wanting to change, Sadie was the first person to go around the place and gather up enough funds so Zara could feel like herself.

It took a while, up to a good 3 to 4 years before it was all saved up and ready for Zara to use. No one was allowed to touch the contents of this fund. Sadie would not have it.

"No one touches this fund. It's for Zara."

To be honest, it would make Zara tear up each time she mentioned about this but she'd become so used to retelling her story that the tears were replaced with smiles. She didn't want to be upset anymore. There was no point in that.

Instead, Zara was looking forward to happy times ahead of her with her friends and found family. This prompted her to go visit Sadie to say thanks to her for letting Zara be her.

She made her way to the gay bar that Sadie worked and looked into the place where she went to when things got tough at home. She noticed the bar tender cleaning away the glasses behind the counter. Best to leave them to it.

Ollie noticed Zara and smiled towards her "Girl! Look at you now!"

Zara let out a smile towards the towering lion "Hi Ollie!"

Ollie took one look at his friend "Honey, you look stunning… wait til mama see's you now, miss!"

"That's why I'm here," Zara explained "I wanted to talk to her, to thank her."

"Of course! She's in her office hun."

Zara thanked Ollie as she made her way at the back of the stage and into a small area where Sadie's office was situated and knocked on the door.

"If that's Cal, I'm smashing your face in again! Damn sleeping around with custo-" Sadie finished her rant as she opened the door and looked up. Zara stood there with a large smile on her face.

"Hi mama!"

"Zara!" the marmoset instantly hugged the poodle girl tightly as she smiled towards her.

"Let me have a good look at you, young lady!" Sadie said as she took Zara's new body in perspective. She'd gone through a lot and Sadie couldn't help but be protective of the young girl.

"Everything's all done now mama, I'm officially a lady now."

"Good," Sadie smiled towards Zara as her ear twitched "So, how's everything been with you, eh?"

Zara giggled "Where do I begin, mama? Asides from the operation and hormones, everything else has been real good. Not so much with family but I'm just happy to be here again with all of you girls."

"I get you, I know that you're family haven't been too supportive but at least you have us, sweetie," Sadie said with a smile towards Zara.

"Yeah, it's just nice to come back and be myself," Zara said.

Sadie nodded as she shuffled through some papers "Well, I best get back in case the others get their panties in a twist. It's so good to see you again though Zara. You know, you can come back whenever you want to."

Zara nodded "I know."

The two ladies made their way out of the offices which Sadie locked behind her and headed out to the front of the stage. Some of the others were waiting at the tables to see Zara come out with Sadie and they all cheered her on.

Zara let out a beautiful smile towards the whole community. They didn't have to do this but it was their choice. She was still part of the family, despite the long year she'd taken to have her operation. It was a nice feeling to come back.

Dan, Ollie, Pete and even Cal gave her a big hug afterwards along with a chaste kiss on her head.

She felt at home again.

Main Character Bio's

<u>Toby the bat</u>

Toby the bat is a 21 year old brown bat that works in the same café as his friend, Dusty the bull. Whilst Toby may act with an indifferent attitude towards others, he is non-judgemental and can take as good as he gives. His non-biased attitude makes him get along with most people but he can be a little aloof at times with his attitude. Even though he may act like this, he is also one of the types to laugh off most jokes made about his straight-faced attitude towards life. Due to his inexperience in love, Toby can get flattered by women easily and finds it hard to talk to them (unless he's had a few alcoholic drinks). Toby is heterosexual and doesn't really care who you are or what you identify as, as long as you're nice towards another person. His love interest is Felicia the bat.

<u>Dusty the bull</u>

Dusty is a 23 year old light brown bull with a warm and loving heart. He is best friends with Toby the bat and tries to encourage his friend to smile and laugh a bit more. Whilst Toby is the straight-faced guy, Dusty is more open and free with his emotions and how he views life. Whilst he displays a rather carefree and loving personality, Dusty can get flustered about sexual matters such as intercourse. He tries his best to inspire others (mostly Toby) to do their best and to develop as a person. He is heterosexual and shows no prejudice towards others who are different from himself. A surprising fact about Dusty is a friends with benefits relationship he has with a cow girl which he openly admits but gets embarrassed when it is brought up.

<u>Felicia the bat</u>

Felicia is a white coloured female bat and is 21 years old. She is good friends with Dusty. She is caring, kind and likes to make sure people have a good time. She can sometimes doubt a person based on her own past experience with an ex-boyfriend, but she learns a lot from a person when they show her something surprising. She loves to have a laugh and have a good time. She is Heterosexual and is best friends with Zara the poodle. She is also the love interest of Toby the bat.

Zara the poodle

Zara the poodle is a 20 year old white coloured poodle who is best friends with Felicia. She is shy when people first meet her but opens up to others in a relatively short space of time. She is also known to be a flirt towards men and make them flustered. People in a local gay bar know her past and still treat her like the lady that she is. She is a fully transitioned trans-woman with attraction to men.

Pete the rhino

Pete is a 27 year old grey skinned rhinoceros who works at a gay club as a drag queen. He is a friendly person with a bubbly personality when out in the streets and with new people he meets, despite his overall appearance being rather menacing. He belongs to a small biker gang who accept him for who he is and are proud of what he does on stage. He is gay and has a boyfriend called Eddy who is a Hippopotamus. They have been together for 6 years.

Eddy the Hippo

Eddy is a 26 year old greyish pink hippo who is a social worker for children. He is a friendly person towards others and likes to be able to make people feel at ease. He is rather homely likes to hug people. He is gay and has a boyfriend called Pete the rhino.

<u>Sadie the Marmoset</u>

Sadie is a 45 year old marmoset who works at the gay club Pete works in. She is head of the entire club and everyone who works there calls her "Mama", due to her mother-hen like personality. She never refuses anyone for help (unless they do something wrong in a bad way) and often acts behind a strong but stern attitude towards her boys. Due to a troubled past, she understands the importance of bringing people together. She wears a black ring on her middle finger on her right hand, indicating her asexuality. She is aromantic but she does have aesthetic attraction towards both genders.

Acknowledgements

There are lots of people I can thank for making me realise that writing a book isn't that hard and putting the dedication to writing is the best thing to do. So for this, let's start off small and work my way up.

I definitely want to say thanks to the staff at the English department of Huddersfield University for being able to put up with the fact they had a blank slate of a person, as I trundled my ass off trying to understand the weird and wonderful world of linguistics and storytelling. To all the students in the same year as me who may not have gotten to known me as well but they have been fantastic people in my life who take the time to listen to each other. You guys are fantastic.

I want to have a special thank you to Michael Stewart who was one of my many teachers who taught me the importance of character building and how to set out a book the correct way. Hope I made you proud, Michael!

Another special thank you is Stephen Ely, a wonderful poet of a man and one who did help to inspire some of my work. Thanks for the inspiration, Stephen!

I have to give the biggest thanks to AVEN who have been a big support during the times I had no idea who I was and what I wanted to be. They were the first people to kind of nudge my stubborn ass in the right direction and tell me "You're Asexual, deal with it!"

(Only kidding, love you guys!")

The real important people I have to thank is my mum and my sister.

My mum has been the woman that has been my rock for the 30 years I have been here. There were times that shit hits the fan and I had no idea what was going on in the world but the lady brought me back to earth. She was the first person I told that I was asexual and took it in her stride.

My sister, although our relationship has been turbulent at times, keeps my head up and tells me how much of a writer I am and sometimes I don't believe it. Now that I have written this, she's right. Thanks love!

This is for all those in and out the closet, wardrobe and other creepy places people like to hang out at; the ones people miss and leave behind. It's for those who haven't had much of a voice because everyone else did the talking for them. The misfits who call themselves mad because their meaning in life is a lot older than what they actually want.

This book is for you.

Don't miss out!

Visit the website below and you can sign up to receive emails whenever Jade Gace publishes a new book. There's no charge and no obligation.

https://books2read.com/r/B-A-KWWCB-MPBUC

BOOKS 2 READ

Connecting independent readers to independent writers.

About the Author

An Aromantic Aseexual who has recently graduated the University of Huddersfield.

This is her first book.

www.ingramcontent.com/pod-product-compliance
Lightning Source LLC
Chambersburg PA
CBHW061303140726
47998CB00006B/2342